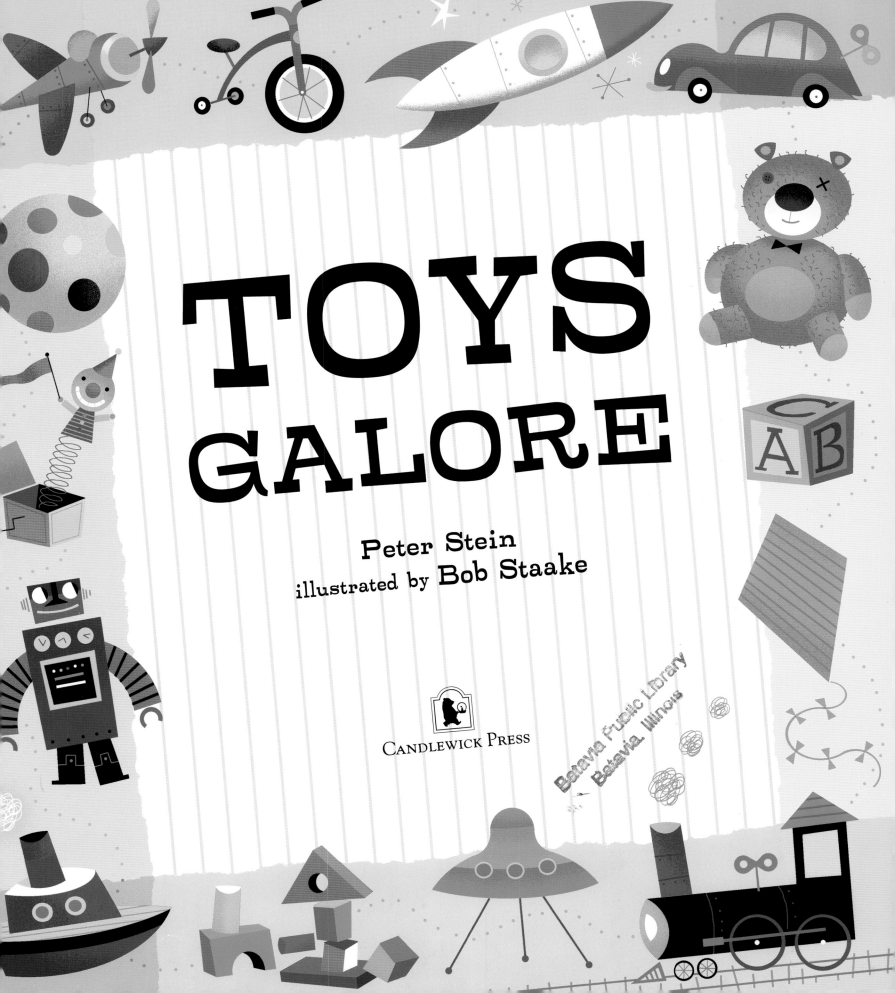

TOYS GALORE

Peter Stein

illustrated by Bob Staake

CANDLEWICK PRESS

Toys are silly.
Toys are fun.
Who loves toys?
Everyone!

THIS toy has
a lot of flair.
What other kinds
of toys are there?
It's good to know!
And nice to share.

Round toy, square toy,
dirt toy, air toy.
Spring toy, string toy.
What-a-THING toy!

Small toy, tall toy,
bouncing-ball toy.
Hat toy, shoe toy.
Stretchy GOO toy!

Toys and MORE toys!
Sandy shore toys!

Climb-it, find-it,
let's-explore toys!

A silly city
made of blocks.
A romping robot
cardboard box.

Puppet creatures
made of socks!

Pots-and-pans toys.
Use-your-hands toys.

Sharing-secrets-
with-tin-cans toys!

Squishy clay, you're fun to play with, squeeze and squash and sculpt all day with!

Toys for teatime,
fun time, free time.
Bouncing knees are
toys for WHEEEE time!

Zippy-quick
remote-control toys!

Jumpin', blastin'
rock 'n' roll toys!

Fairies, gnomes,
and ugly troll toys!

Floaty, bubbly,
while-you-wash toys.

Struggling, juggling,
OH-MY-GOSH toys!

Toys and toys and zillions MORE toys! Whirling, twirling toys-GALORE toys!

Jump toys! Ride toys!
Slip-and-slide toys!
Up-and-down and
side-to-side toys!

Toys for one
and toys for all.
Ping-Pong, jacks,
and basketball.

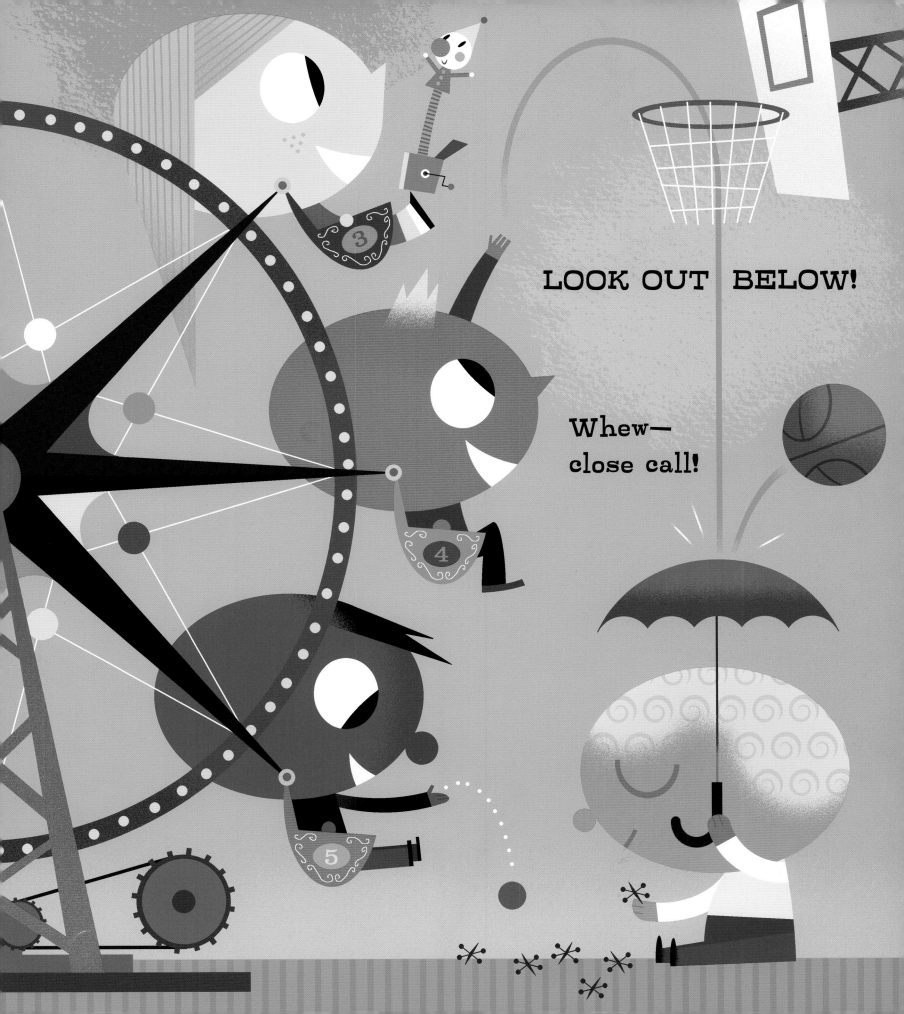

LOOK OUT BELOW!

Whew—
close call!

Creaky, squeaky
old-time race car.
Futuristic
outer-space car!
Soap Box Derby
homemade chase car!

What are these toys?
Floaty breeze toys!
What are those toys?
Soak-your-clothes toys!

What is THAT toy?
It's a splat toy!

Toys in pairs.
Toys on stairs.

Looks like this toy
needs repairs.

Muddy toys in
messy puddles.
Snuggly toys for
hugging cuddles.

But which toy is
the best toy ever?
The one most fun?
Most cool and clever?

It can't be found
inside a store
or in a box
or in a drawer
or in your room
or on a shelf.

No, this toy's found
inside *yourself.*
It's there—right now!
A toy SENSATION!

Your very own
imagination.

For Lois, Amy, and Jon
P. S.

To Y
B. S.

Text copyright © 2013 by Peter Stein
Illustrations copyright © 2013 by Bob Staake

First edition 2013

Library of Congress Catalog Card Number 2012947733
ISBN 978-0-7636-6254-7

13 14 15 16 17 18 LEO 10 9 8 7 6 5 4 3 2 1

Printed in Heshan, Guangdong, China

This book was typeset in Zalderdash.
The illustrations were created digitally.

Candlewick Press
99 Dover Street
Somerville, Massachusetts 02144

visit us at www.candlewick.com